The Chinese

L. Newton Hayes

Alpha Editions

This edition published in 2024

ISBN : 9789367247020

Design and Setting By
Alpha Editions
www.alphaedis.com
Email - info@alphaedis.com

As per information held with us this book is in Public Domain.
This book is a reproduction of an important historical work. Alpha Editions uses the best technology to reproduce historical work in the same manner it was first published to preserve its original nature. Any marks or number seen are left intentionally to preserve its true form.

Contents

INTRODUCTION .... - 3 -
PREFACE .... - 4 -
CHAPTER ONE THE PLACE OF THE DRAGON
IN CHINESE LIFE... - 8 -
CHAPTER TWO HOW THE DRAGON IDEA
ORIGINATED.. - 12 -
CHAPTER THREE THE VARIETIES OF DRAGONS......... - 15 -
CHAPTER FOUR WHAT DRAGONS REALLY
LOOK LIKE... - 20 -
CHAPTER FIVE PEOPLE WHO HAVE SEEN DRAGONS - 26 -
CHAPTER SIX THE DRAGON IN WESTERN
MYTHOLOGY .... - 30 -
CHAPTER SEVEN QUAINT BELIEFS ABOUT
THE DRAGON .... - 34 -
CHAPTER EIGHT HOW DRAGONS CONTROL THE
FORTUNES OF MEN .... - 37 -
CHAPTER NINE THE HOLD OF THE DRAGON
ON CHINA.. - 41 -

BRONZE DRAGON, KANG HSI PERIOD

Three hundred years ago Pèro Veribest, Jesuit priest at the court of Kang Hsi, cast a number of bronze astronomical instruments for his imperial patron. The apparatus, of which this is a part, stands in the open, but the workmanship is so perfect and the care it has received has been so faithful that one would hardly imagine that this dragon was cast more than three centuries ago.

DRAGON COLONNADE AT CHUFU

Ten stately stone columns in the portico before the Confucian Temple at Chufu, Shantung. This temple stands near two of China's most sacred shrines, the sites of the birthplace and of the grave of China's greatest sage. The pillars are monoliths of white marble, nearly twenty feet in height. These are decorated with huge dragons in deep relief. This is said to be the most perfect and most beautiful stone colonnade in China.

INTRODUCTION

The subject of this little book is of general interest to people who are acquainted with things Chinese. The dragon has played a large part in Chinese thought through four thousand and more years. Even in these days of the Republic it still fills an important place in Chinese life.

The dragon is one of the most common ornamental designs in China and one meets it wherever one goes in this country. However, in spite of the significance attached to the dragon, very little has ever been written concerning it in either Chinese or English. Only a few general articles on this subject have been published in magazines, and the references to it in books are very brief. No independent study of the dragon in book form has been made in either of these two languages until now.

The author is peculiarly fitted to undertake this piece of work. He was born in China and speaks the Chinese language as a native. Thus he has had the first-hand knowledge and the language to help him in his study. He has been studying on the subject of the dragon for fourteen years. In this time he has traveled over more than one half the number of provinces of China. The study is therefore not the result of a few month's investigation, nor is it the product of research in only one city or province. The author's acquaintance with the people and the language of China have made it possible for him to go to original sources and to study the subject from every angle Perhaps the last word on the Chinese dragon is not yet said, nevertheless it is safe to say that this treatise is as complete as our present knowledge will permit. This little volume should be of value to all who are interested in China.

This account of the dragon will not only be of value to foreigners, but it will also be such to Chinese. The author has made this study a hobby for many years and the result of his research is a splendid contribution to the literature on China. It would be a good idea for more people to take up the study of other phases of Chinese life in the same way and thus help to interpret China to the West.

FONG F. SEC.

May 9, 1922.

PREFACE

In the spring of 1909 the writer had the honor of being a guest for a week in the summer home of Dr. W. A. P. Martin, near Peking. Many residents of the Capital during the decade preceding the Revolution, and for a number of years before that, knew "Pearl Grotto" and visited the venerable senior missionary of China, then lately retired from the Presidency of the Imperial Tung Wen College.

Dr. Martin was a scholar of the old school and enjoyed few pursuits better than that of reviewing his remarkable memory of the classical writers. During the meals the old gentleman, then nearly eighty, would quote readily from Homer, Horace, and Virgil, and would ask his guest to translate the passages freely into English and to cite the books and chapters quoted.

After a few days in this uncomfortable situation the guest began to cast about for some means of relief. At that time he had been in the country but a few months, and was just beginning a general study of Chinese art. The dragon, among other objects of interest, particularly attracted his attention. It occurred to him to ask Dr. Martin some questions about this creature whose form was so popular with the Chinese. Accordingly a carefully prepared list of six or seven questions about the dragon was launched one morning across the breakfast table before the attack of Greek and Latin began. The first question met with a noncommittal reply, the second fared little better, and so on to the end. Then Dr. Martin admitted that this was one of the subjects about which he knew very little. He was, however, very warm in his desire to help find answers to these questions, and he referred his guest to his personal friend, Sir Robert Hart, the Inspector General of the Imperial Customs, who had also lived fifty years in China. Unfortunately Sir Robert's replies were as vague as those of the retired Professor. The questions which were asked of these two eminent Sinologues were also submitted to several other British and Americans in Peking, and later to many Chinese, but with similar results.

It soon became evident that if the searcher for light on "Things Chinese" were to learn much about this creature which had challenged his attention, he must look it up from original sources. He was later convinced of this fact when he found it impossible to secure any satisfactory information from books published in English. He then resolved that before he himself was fifteen years in the country he would have answers to the seven questions which he had asked of his friends in Peking. The contents of this brochure are the results of a study made in ten provinces of China over a period of fourteen years. While this volume is not offered as the final word upon this subject, it probably represents the most exhaustive study thus far given to the Chinese dragon.

This book is not intended primarily for Sinologues and it contains no Chinese characters. The volume is written for the average reader, who in his study of things Chinese, has little time to go to original sources. Most people do not wish to be burdened with long quotations to prove abstract hypotheses or to have Chinese characters inserted in the text repeatedly to break the sequence.

If later interest in this subject justifies it, a larger work will be attempted and a more detailed presentation of the material thus far collected will be made. The writer's purpose in this book has been to make as clear a statement of the subject as could be done within the compass of a small book, without introducing unnecessary material. If he has succeeded in this endeavor, he will be more than gratified.

EMPEROR KANG HSI IN DRAGON ROBES

Kang Hsi, the venerated patron of art and literature, died at the age of sixty-nine, after ruling China for sixty-one years. This portrait was painted in the Imperial Palace at Peking, shortly before he died in 1723.

THE DRAGON THRONE OF THE RECENT EMPERORS

This massive structure, surmounted by countless dragons, stands in the Imperial Palace in Peking. From the dragon throne issued the decrees which, before the Republic, controlled the destinies of one quarter of the human race.

CHAPTER ONE
THE PLACE OF THE DRAGON IN CHINESE LIFE

There are real dragons living in China to-day. These are not the horrible monsters that some have imagined them to be. They are friendly creatures highly revered by all the people. They possess marvelous powers and they occasionally permit themselves to be seen by mortal eyes. Such is the belief of at least seven out of every ten Chinese.

The popular belief in the dragon is so deeply rooted and so widespread that it is advisable for one to secure an accurate knowledge of the Chinese idea of the venerated saurian if he desires to gain a truly sympathetic understanding of this remarkable people. Nearly every phase of Chinese life bears evidence of the influence of this unique member of the animal kingdom. Particularly is this true in the realms of their art, literature, folklore, zoölogy, history, and religion.

Chinese art employs dragon designs in endless variety. The graceful lines of its symmetrically proportioned body are found in every part of the country painted upon silks and porcelain, woven into brocades, carved on wood, embroidered upon satin, cast in bronze, and chiseled upon marble. It is the most characteristically Chinese of the many Oriental designs which are so attractive to Western students of art.

The literature of the country abounds in references to this marvelous creature as one may readily discover by even a cursory study of its books of history, poetry, letters, medicine, and fiction.

Chinese folklore is replete with countless entertaining stories of the wonderful feats of this great animal, while an infinite number of proverbs and old folks' sayings bear their testimony to the almost universal belief in its existence.

Popular zoölogy places the dragon next to man, at the head of the list of all living creatures, thus occupying the position of the lion or tiger in our Western classification. Strictly speaking, Chinese natural history gives the dragon the rank of king only of scale-covered animals or creatures which live in the sea; the two fabulous creatures, the Chi Ling and the Phœnix respectively, have first place above all beasts and other animals which live upon the earth, and all birds and other creatures which fly in the air. But because the dragon is equally at home in the air and on the earth, as well as in the sea, it has been ranked as the ruler of all created life below man.

Chinese geomancy for ages has looked to the dragon as a means of determining the fates and fortunes of the "Sons of Han." Until very recently comparatively few Chinese would build a house or bury a corpse without first consulting a geomancer, who would, in one way or another, refer to its probable influence upon his action. It is, moreover, a generally accepted belief that every twelfth hour, day, month, and year of the lunar calendar are under the dragon's dominating control.

Chinese history records scores of appearances of the king of beasts through the four thousand or more years since the age of the three mythical rulers. Appearances of the dragon are connected with the stories of many prominent characters of China's past. Perhaps the most noteworthy reference is one which states that two dragons as guards of honor visited the home of Confucius on the day that great sage was born. These frequent references to the dragon are considered, for the most part, by the majority of Chinese scholars quite as authentic as the statements about the famous worthies themselves.

Chinese religion places the dragon in the calendar of its deities as the God of Rain and the Ruler of Rivers, Lakes, and Seas. As such it has been worshiped for centuries. There are probably very few cities of any size in the whole country which, at least until the recent revolution, were without a temple or shrine to the dragon king. This deity was worshiped on the first and fifteenth of every month.

In the opinion of the writer dwellers in other lands commonly think of the dragon in much the same light as they think of the centaurs, of Geryon or the Minotaur of Grecian fables: a strange mythical creature merely the product of human fancy. It is also probable that most of them think that the majority of Chinese consider it in the same way, but this is a mistaken conception. It may be considered a very conservative estimate to state that at least three hundred and sixty million Chinese believe in the actual existence of dragons as firmly as other peoples believe that there are such animals as tigers roaming in the jungles of Bengal and such monsters as walruses wandering over the icy stretches which border the arctic circle, though they themselves may never have set foot upon the shores of India nor have crossed the Arctic Sea.

The Han Dynasty Dragons

The brick upon which these dragons are molded was baked two thousand years ago. It was dug up recently near Kaifengfu, in Honan province, one of the ancient capitals of China. When two dragons appear in art they usually face each other. On this ancient brick the reverse is true. The circle through which these animals have wound themselves has become, in modern art, a disk. Most dragons are portrayed gazing intently at the disk, which is usually described as the sun. The simplicity of these dragons is very marked in contrast to the elaborate designs of the present day.

The Porcelain Dragon Screen

Nine huge dragons of many colors disport themselves upon this imperial screen. It is approximately one hundred feet long and twenty feet high. This impressive structure, faced with porcelain tiles of the finest texture, stands on the edge of the "North Sea," within the walls of the Imperial Palace in Peking.

Quite recently the writer made a localized study of the universality of the belief in dragons. One hundred representative Chinese of different ages and walks in life in an important city were asked the following questions: Do you believe in the present existence of the dragon? And what percentage of the people of China do you think hold this belief? Eighty-two of the one hundred answered the first question in the affirmative. Regarding the universality of the belief in the dragon these men estimated that at least eighty-six and six-tenths per cent of their fellow nationals believe in its existence. The above study bore out very accurately the writer's estimate of the extent of the popular belief in the dragon. His judgment was based upon questions asked many scores of Chinese in ten different provinces of the country through a period of fourteen years.

CHAPTER TWO
HOW THE DRAGON IDEA ORIGINATED

The elaborate conception of the dragon which we find to-day in Chinese art and literature is undoubtedly a very different animal from the one which was responsible for the origin of the dragon idea. The fabled sea serpent, the alligator, the salamander, and the boa constrictor have each been regarded as the prototype of this unique creature. It is far more likely, however, that some antediluvian saurian was the true source from which the dragon idea has sprung. Back in the dawn of history some early member of the human race may have met with one of these monstrous creatures which paleontologists tell us were, in some period of their development, equally at home on land and in the sea, and because of its gigantic size and marvelous powers attributed to it a supernatural origin. In later ages, even the unearthed skeleton of one of these monsters might have been sufficient to have led to the inception of the story. If this theory is correct it is easy to understand how through succeeding ages the belief could have grown and how superstition and coincidence would have done their share to elaborate from the early monster the marvelous creature of the present day.

According to the theory advanced above, the writer believes that the most probable prototype of the dragon is the Brontosaurus of the Mesozoic age, although the present conception of the dragon may easily have sprung from such other prehistoric animals, as the plesiosaurus of the same period or the Iguanodon of the Cenozoic age. Skeletons of these giants of the saurian family and pictures of the reconstructed animals indicate a striking resemblance to the graceful creatures that dominate the art of China.

The first appearance of the true dragon, according to the records of what is considered to be authentic Chinese history, occurred some forty-six centuries ago during the reign of Huang Ti, or Hsuan Yuan, the third of the five great rulers. We are told that after this personage had reigned one hundred and eleven years a large dragon appeared and took him to heaven upon his back. Since that day dragons have been seen in every dynasty and by hundreds of witnesses, as Chinese history abundantly attests. Dragon appearances were considered auspicious, and augured well for the affairs of state. In support of this belief, it is interesting to note that when the late President Yuan Shih-kai was trying to make himself emperor his friends made at least one attempt to unearth what were supposed to be the bones of a dragon. This was done in order that the superstitious among his countrymen might be led to feel that his desire to reëstablish the empire was according to the law of heaven.

For centuries it was the custom for anyone who saw a dragon, either himself or through the magistrate of the district in which he lived, immediately to announce the fact to the emperor. In early days history was often counted from the appearance of a particular dragon.

A popular fable relates that Yü Wang was able to end the great flood 2297 B.C. only after he had succeeded in capturing the dragon, who was said to be responsible for the deluge. The animal was chained in heavy irons and imprisoned, after which the flood subsided. Ever since that time all dragons, we are told, have trembled at the memory of the only man who ever conquered their kind.

THE DRAGON STAIRCASE

In most Confucian and imperial temples the center of the path that leads from the temple entrance to the sacred shrine is known as the spirit way. Where this route leads up a staircase, one usually finds not steps but a large inclined stone on which are carved one or more dragons. At the hour of worship the spirit of the one who is honored, travels, we are told, over this course. The dragon monolith shown in this photograph leads up to the smallest, the central one, of the three altars at the Temple of Heaven in Peking.

AN IMPERIAL DRAGON

This lifelike creature, symbolic of imperial power, adorns one of the walls within the palace ground of Peking. Here, as in most representations, the dragon is shown gazing longingly at the flaming sun. He desires, we are told, not so much to seize that heavenly body as to learn the secret of its brilliance, so that it may add to his own glory.

CHAPTER THREE
THE VARIETIES OF DRAGONS

To the majority of people the word "dragon" denotes one animal only. There are, however, at least eight species of animals which bear this name. These are the Lung Wang, the Shen Lung, the Li Lung, the Chiao Lung, the Ying Lung, the Chiu Lung, the Tsao Lung, and the Tu Lung. They all belong to the genus dragon (Lung), but each has one or more characteristics which differentiates it from the others. For example, the Li Lung, or Chih Lung, as it is also named, has and is the only species which possesses wings. It is, however, but one of these species, the Shen Lung, which will be considered at this time. Of the eight varieties this is the one best known. The others may be dismissed with a word. Dr. Williams, in his "Middle Kingdom," mentions only three varieties and says that these are respectively dragons of the sky, of the sea, and of marshes. However, it seems that the Chinese are not generally accustomed to make such a classification. They rather consider that the one species, Shen Lung, controls and operates in all of these three spheres. Most of the other varieties are minor creatures which are practically unknown and have slight bearing upon this study. The one exception to this rule is the Lung Wang, or dragon king. This species differs from the others in that its members possess a dragon's head upon a human body. By some this dragon is said to answer to Neptune in Western mythology. Each ocean has a dragon king. The members of this species differ from those of the one in which we are the most interested in that dragon kings rarely grow old and never die. The remaining varieties are all quite secondary and practically never appear in any form of art. These are mentioned only occasionally in Chinese literature. This article will therefore be confined to an account of the Shen Lung, or spirit dragon, the real dragon, the dragon which has held China in its spell since the days of Yao and Shun.

TABLET TO CONFUCIUS

This red lacquer tablet, inscribed with eight characters in gold, stands in the shrine of the Provincial Temple of Chekiang at Hangchow. The inscription may be freely translated, "The Sacred Tablet of Our Revered Teacher Confucius." The tablet is approximately four feet high and one foot wide. Nine dragons play hide and seek in the framework that borders the edge of the inscription. Two larger dragons twine themselves about the slender pillars before the shrine. These serve as guards of honor. These two creatures symbolize the two dragons which, history says, encircled the home of Confucius when the sage was born. Similar tablets are found in all temples to Confucius throughout China.

Dragon Gateway

Within the main entrance to Nanking's Examination Hall, where the Master's Degree was earned, stood a long "spirit wall." Upon the front of this structure was painted a dragon gate, beneath which was shown a carp changing into a dragon. A Bachelor of Arts, according to China's ancient system of education, upon becoming a Master, was congratulated by his friends as having passed through the "Dragon Gate." The implication was that it was as difficult for a Bachelor of Arts to become a Master as for a carp to be transformed into a dragon.

All true dragons are of two kinds: those which are such by birth and those which become dragons by transformation from fish of the carp species. The transformed variety become dragons by leaping up the waters of a certain cataract upon a western mountain stream. Large numbers of carp swim once each year, we learn, to this waterfall known as the "Dragon's Gate." Here under the cataract they flounder about, jumping and springing up out of the swirling waters; a few of them succeed in getting over the falls to the higher waters above. Those which are successful in this effort become dragons. After the story of this strange occurrence became known to the public, it was incorporated into the life of the people in a popular saying, and scholars who succeeded in passing the great triennial literary examinations were said to have "passed the Dragon Gate." The use of this figure was doubtless to illustrate the difficulty of passing the examinations, for it implied that it was as difficult a task for a man to succeed at these examinations as it was for the carp to leap up over the falls. This figure has, in addition, the happy inference that even as the carp, an ordinary fish, might become a mighty dragon, just so by this supreme effort a scholar might become a master of arts, thus placing the value of the transformation on a very high scale.

One ancient authority tells us that there is a class of these great saurians which are known as "lazy dragons." These do not like to exert themselves in the task of directing clouds which carry rain over the surface of the earth. They sometimes make themselves small in size, drop to the surface of the earth and hide in trees, under roofs of houses, and even in the clothing of unsuspecting countrymen. The Thunder God, learning of their desertion from their posts of duty, sends his messengers to search for them and when he discovers their location, kills them with thunderbolts during an electric storm, after the manner of Zeus. This explains to many an unsophisticated man the frequent destruction of life and property during thunderstorms. An epithet that in some parts of the country is often hurled at lazy people is "Lan Lung," or "lazy dragon."

THE DRAGON STONE

In the city of Kaifengfu, Honan, the first capital of the Sung emperors, is a sacred building known as the "Dragon Pavilion." Within this structure, which stands on an eminence high above most of the buildings of the city, is a large basaltic stone known as the "Dragon Throne." This is cut in the form of a cube of about six feet in each dimension and rests to-day under the shrine of the Pearly Emperor. Nine hundred years ago the Sung emperors doubtlessly placed their lacquered thrones upon its upper surface. In order to protect it from vandal hands, the historic stone is now incased within wooden walls, which form a cavelike room about it. Fourteen dragons in deep relief surround the outer edge: five on the front and back faces, and two on either end. Visitors must use candles in order to see at all in the inky darkness. Because of the narrow quarters no photograph can be taken. This drawing by a Kaifengfu artist was made under the greatest difficulties and is probably the first reproduction ever attempted.

DRAGON EAVES TILE

This crescent-shaped tile fell from the roof of one of the imperial temples of Peking. It is made of highly glazed porcelain and is ten inches across and five inches high. Its age is estimated to be about two hundred years.

CHAPTER FOUR
WHAT DRAGONS REALLY LOOK LIKE

Comparatively few Chinese of the older generation seem to question the existence of dragons or to doubt the marvelous powers usually attributed to them. In view of this fact it is surprising to find how ignorant is the average person who holds this belief when asked to give an accurate description of the great creature. Perhaps this is not strange, however, when we remember that there are apparently no books which purport to give any complete account of the dragon. The innumerable references to it in Chinese literature largely deal with the dragon's performances and say little about his appearance. In order to make a satisfactory study of the dragon one must, therefore, follow a tedious process of collecting, eliminating, and coördinating a multitude of stories, proverbs, and incidents from history, and make a careful study of selected pictures and carvings, and if possible secure interviews with those who profess to have seen the great king of the animal creation.

One writer, who is anxious to make intelligible to the average person the accepted representation of the king of all created life below man, describes the dragon in terms of animals with many of which we are quite familiar. He says that it has the head of a camel, the horns of a deer, the ears of a cow, the neck of a snake, the body of a fish, the scales of a carp, the claws of an eagle, the eyes of a devil, and the paws of a tiger.

The bodies of all dragons, we are informed, are symmetrically divided into three sections of equal length, these divisions being from the point of the nose to the shoulders, from the shoulders to the thighs, and from the thighs to the tip of the tail.

DRAGON-GUARDED ASTROLABE

This exquisitely wrought bronze instrument for measuring the position of the stars may be seen in Peking. It stands at the foot of the ramp leading to the Imperial Observatory. Three hundred years ago the Jesuit astronomer Veribest had this, and a score of other magnificent instruments, cast for the emperor Kang Hsi. Most of these great pieces are surmounted or protected by dragons of the finest workmanship.

SURROUNDED BY DRAGONS

This palace portrait was a prized possession of the Manchu emperors. Yung Cheng, the son of Kang Hsi, is here shown upon the throne, which he ascended in 1723. Countless dragons disport themselves upon his costly robes of state and writhe and wreathe themselves in the lattice structure of his imperial throne.

The "Shoh Wen," a book written during the Tang dynasty, says that the dragon has the following marvelous powers: "It may cause itself to become visible or invisible at will, and it can become long or short, and coarse or fine, at its own good pleasure." This wonderful versatility, of course, makes it difficult for us to find any recorded statement of the maximum length of this creature, since there is no limit set for its expansion. Another book of the Tang dynasty helps out a little, however, when it describes a certain dragon, which was found dead, as having been over one hundred feet long, while other accounts lead us to believe that the dragon at times assumes a size several miles in length. The smallest size of which any statement has been found was the length of a silkworm.

In color, dragons are differentiated as being red, yellow, blue, white, or black. During the Manchu dynasty, yellow was the imperial color, and the yellow or golden dragon was designated the imperial dragon. In the preceding dynasty, the Ming dynasty, when red was the national color, it is believed that the red dragon was proclaimed, by decree of the emperor, the official dragon of the empire.

Every careful observer in the Far East has noticed a difference in the number of claws in the pictures of dragons—some possessing three, others four, and still others five claws. The smallest number is found on the dragons of Japanese art. Ordinarily Chinese dragons have four claws, while those of five were recognized as imperial dragons. The two types of Chinese dragons, with these slight variations, are, however, one and the same species, and are identical in every other respect. An attempt has been made to prove that the variation of claws from three through four to five is a historic development, but we can find no conclusive proof to substantiate this theory. It is possible that the ancient dragon designs of China have only three claws on each foot. Japan borrowed her art from China, and it is not unlikely that at the period when she borrowed this design the Chinese dragon was represented with only three claws.

It is said of the carp that it always has exactly thirty-six scales in each row, leading from its head to its tail. After the same manner, dragons are described as possessing eighty-one scales in each series.

The true dragon has nine sons. Each is different in appearance from the other and each possesses his own peculiar characteristics. These children of the dragon are the variants in appearance from the general line which we are accustomed to look for in the dragon, and which we often see in carvings and architecture. The dragon heads on bells, on the peak tiles of temples and palaces, on sword hilts, on monuments, and in similar places are representations of the progeny of the God of Rain and do not portray that god himself.

A Dragon-Mounted Bell

Three dragons unite themselves to form the structure from which hangs this graceful bell. The frame is of redwood from southern China and, like much of the carvings from the city of Foochow, it is richly inlaid with silver. A fourth dragon coils over the surface of the bell. Two dragonlike heads unite to form the loop by which the bell is hung. These represent one variety of the nine sons of the king of the animal world.

A CLOUD DRAGON

One of the men who claimed to have seen a living dragon was by profession an artist. This medallion was drawn by him. "Except for the whiskers, this painting represents what I saw when a young man in Shantung province." The cloud dragon is a favorite theme of artists. Dragons are supposed to travel about upon the clouds. It is a common belief, and one which was held also by Confucius, that clouds spring from dragons. An ancient and well-known saying declares: "Clouds come from dragons and wind from tigers."

CHAPTER FIVE
PEOPLE WHO HAVE SEEN DRAGONS

In spite of the fact that modern zoölogy has never included in the pages of its textbooks descriptions and pictures of the dragon as a creature of reality, yet there are men in China to-day who claim to have seen these animals, some of which have been described very accurately. The writer has had the pleasure of conversing with several Chinese who assert that they have seen the dragon at close range. He has also secured, at secondhand, information from others who are said to have looked upon this most marvelous of creatures. All of the men whom the writer interviewed were of sound mind and were accredited by their acquaintances with being men of reliable character. There is no reason to believe that any one of them were inebriate or under the power of hallucination at the time they witnessed the creatures of their description.

A teacher in a Tientsin school related that he once saw a dragon in his native province, Shantung. The animal had been killed, so it was believed, by the order of heaven, as a punishment for some misdeed, and had fallen to the earth, where it lay as the center of attraction for hundreds of people who came in crowds from that whole countryside. Its appearance was identical with that of the popular pictures with which we are familiar. A school servant, who was also a native of Shantung, and whose home was near the sea, declared that he once saw a dragon. He told the writer that it was about fifteen feet long and that it fell to the earth during a severe rainstorm. It, too, attracted a large crowd of spectators. Although this man was unable to give very satisfactory details, yet his unusual earnestness and apparent sincerity were convincing evidence that he had really seen a monster of a remarkable type.

A third person, an elderly gentleman, who is a teacher of classics in one of the schools of Nanking, informed the writer that when he was a young man a dragon fell one night from the sky and lay for twenty-four hours near his home. The country folk respectfully covered it with matting, but he managed to raise the covering and saw its great cowlike head, its four legs, and its scale-covered body. It was about fifty feet long and blue in color. As in the other two cases, this dragon disappeared from the earth during a heavy storm. It was generally believed that it came to life again and was taken up into the heavens upon a cloud, which formed beneath its body.

The artist who drew the picture of the cloud dragon recounted that, during the thirty-fourth year of the Emperor Kuang Hsu, while he himself was on his way to Peking to receive the seals of a district magistrate, he came across a dragon lying upon the banks of the Yellow River in Shantung province. It was blue in color and was several tens of feet in length. The whole air was filled with a very offensive salt sea odor, and out of respect for the creature, which was supposed to have fallen from heaven, the crowd of people that stood around was busily engaged in sprinkling water upon its body. The head resembled that of a cow and the artist said that except for the long eyebrows the picture of the cloud dragon represented very faithfully what he actually saw.

Another Chinese has related that a business partner of his, while on a journey up the Yangtze River, saw three dragons crossing a mountain range near the shore. Every person on board was spellbound as they watched the three monsters—one yellow, another white, and the third blue—as they majestically made their way with great undulating strides up the mountain side. The dragons passed by so near the boat that the observers saw every detail of their heads and the lacelike scales of their bodies. The boat was respectfully stopped in mid-river, and only when the dragons had disappeared over the ridge did the boatmen resume their task at the oars.

Various stories have come to the writer, of dragons which have been seen either riding upon banks of fog or dangling from passing clouds during great windstorms or rainstorms. Invariably these have been described as having scale-covered bodies. One reasonable explanation for the suspended dragons may be found in insipient tornadoes and water spouts which never reach the ground. There seems, however, to be no explanation for the dragon visits described by the five observers, unless it be that strange monsters of the deep either crawled up out of the river and lay on the bank, in a dormant state, or were sucked up by ocean- or river-water spouts, and when the columns of water broke over the land the creatures were dropped far from their natural habitat. Two difficulties at once present themselves to combat this hypothesis. The first of these is the improbability that there are such creatures in existence, and the second difficulty lies in the strangeness of their disappearance after coming to the earth. As a possible explanation of the first difficulty, we wish to ask whether it is not possible that there are still existing in the depths of the sea and in great rivers curious reptiles and strange monsters such as no human beings now living have ever seen, the descendants of the mighty saurians which lived upon the earth long ages ago, and which geologists tell us later entered the sea, making that their more secretive habitat?

CIRCULAR DRAGON EAVES TILE

This tile was found in the débris near the Ming Tomb of Nanking. The body of Chu Yuan Chang, the founder of the Ming dynasty and the only emperor buried in the imperial cemetery east of Nanking, was interred about 1399. This tile is of dark yellow porcelain, eight inches in diameter. It is probably five hundred years old.

CHIEN LUNG VASES

These two dainty porcelain vases of the Chien Lung period were "burned" a little over one hundred years ago. The paws of the dragon each contain five claws. Creamy clouds and red flames of fire fill in the background, while conventional green waves decorate the base.

As an explanation for the disappearance of the dragon in these three instances the writer notes two facts. The dragons in each case were seen on the banks of great rivers and in each case disappeared after a heavy rain. Might it not have been that the monsters were in reality not dead but only unconscious, and that the heavy flood washed the creatures back into the river whence they were carried out to sea?

CHAPTER SIX
THE DRAGON IN WESTERN MYTHOLOGY

The dragon is not a conception of the Chinese mind alone. It also occupies a prominent place in the legends and literature of most of the countries of Europe. Cicero in his "de Divinatione" (Book II, line 30), Euripides in his "Philostratus" (Book I, line 2), and Homer in the "Iliad" (Book II, line 309) all mention a dragon.

The Bible, in twenty-two references in the Old Testament and thirteen instances in the New, refers to the dragon either allegorically or as a real animal; however, in many of these passages, especially in the Old Testament, the word "dragon" is an unfortunate rendition, for in several places the writers of the Scriptures very evidently had the conception of an animal that was in all probability the modern jackal.

The myths and legends of Europe have preserved for us numerous dragon stories with which we are more or less familiar. Among others are the tale of Perseus, who rescued Andromeda from a dragon; the story of St. George and the Dragon; the account of Sigfried, who killed a dragon at Worms; and the story of Beowulf, who in the early days of history's dawn dispatched a dragon after slaying Grendel.

King Arthur, who was spoken of as the "dread Pendragon," is described by Tennyson, in his "Idylls of the King," as sitting upon a veritable dragon throne which would vie in splendor with that of China's Manchu emperors. The vivid imagination of the poet laureate gives us this picture:

"To his crown the golden dragon clung

And down his robe the dragon writhed in gold

And from the carven work behind him crept

Two dragons gilded, sloping down to make

Arms to his chair, while all the rest of them

Through knots and loops and folds innumerable,

Fled ever through the woodwork till they found

The new design wherein they lost themselves."

Many coast and river cities of England, France, Italy, and Egypt still proudly recount their local legends of cruel dragons which were slain, after battles royal, upon near-by rivers or in adjacent seas. We may read of the Green Dragon of Mordiford, the Dragon of Norwich, the Great Dragon of Pittempton, the Dragon of Naples, the Dragon of Arles, the Dragon of

Lyons, the Dragon of Marseilles, Sebec, the Dragon of the Nile, and many more. These stories are proudly treasured as the sacred traditions of their respective cities and countries.

The Chinese conception of the dragon presents a very different creature from that of the nations bordering on the Mediterranean and the Atlantic. It is true that there are a few points of similarity, but there is only one to which we shall call attention at this time. That is regarding its keenness of eyesight. Both types are endowed with marvelous vision. The Chinese dragon is deaf and it is explained that its eyes, through natural compensation, have attained an extraordinary power. His vision is so keen that he can easily distinguish a blade of grass one hundred li away. In this connection it is interesting to recall that the English word "dragon" is derived from the Greek "*drakon*" (δράκων), which means "to gaze" or "to see," and the classics more than once refer to the animal as "sharpsighted."

We do not know who first attached the English name "dragon" to the Chinese conception "*lung*," but it is hardly fair to the Oriental ruler of the sea to be branded with the stigma which accompanies the English designation. Since the recent revolution, several devout Westerners have been heard to express their great satisfaction that the dragon flag has now forever disappeared. A misconception of the use of the word "dragon" had caused the speakers to confuse the evil monster mentioned in the book of Revelation with the animal so highly revered by the Chinese. The dragon of the Chinese differs from the generally accepted Western idea in three striking particulars: in appearance, in disposition, and in the regard in which it is held.

In appearance, the European conception varies but slightly from the creature which was its probable prototype, save for the addition of a pair of wings. The Chinese species is developed to a higher degree. The latter has a more massive head from which protrude two branching horns. This species, with the single exception of the Chih Lung, or Li Lung, has no wings but travels from place to place upon the clouds.

A still greater difference between the two varieties exists in the matter of disposition. The European dragon is usually portrayed as a cruel monster, the personification of all that is evil, and the enemy of man. Christian art represents it as opposed to law, harmony, and progress and symbolic of sin and paganism. In this allegorical sense it is painted in struggles with St. George, St. Michael, and St. Sylvester, who personified Christianity and enlightenment. Saints and martyrs are pictured in the process of crushing the dragon beneath their feet. The Chinese dragon, on the other hand, is in this respect very nearly its antithesis. It is a beneficent creature, a friend to man. It brings the rain which produces the crops that in turn supply his food.

The third point of distinction between the two dragons lies in the esteem in which it is held. The Western species was a horrible, loathesome creature, shunned and dreaded by all mortals, while the Asiatic dragon is held in reverence and even worshiped by the Chinese. This creature is in fact so highly revered that one of the most sacred titles which was bestowed upon the emperors was "The True Dragon."

A LIVING DRAGON

Most representations of the dragon indicate peaceful, passive creatures. The artist who designed this dragon for the garden of the emperors at Peking was a master of his art. This graceful creature fairly throbs with life, and we almost hold our breath as we look with the expectation that it will detach itself from the mural background and launch out into space. It is a living thing, and we feel that in another moment it will jerk back its head and rise to disappear before our very eyes.

Two Porcelain Dragons

Of the nine huge saurians that play in the emerald waves beneath the pale blue sky on the imperial screen at Peking, no two assume the same attitude. Leaping, springing, and lunging, each is struggling to reach the sun disk, which lies just out of reach before its face.

CHAPTER SEVEN
QUAINT BELIEFS ABOUT THE DRAGON

"The whiskers of the dragon," according to a book of the Yuan dynasty, "are three feet long and purple in color. If dragon whiskers are mounted upon a crystal handle like a horsehair whip and are placed in a room at night, flies and mosquitoes will not enter." We are further informed that "if this instrument is swished through the air it will make such a noise that chickens, dogs, cows, and horses on hearing it will try to hide. If dragon whiskers are placed in deep water all scale-covered animals will swim immediately to the spot, thinking that their master, the dragon, is there."

A strange fire plays about the body of the dragon. This differs from the fire with which we are familiar in that it blazes brightly when brought into contact with water. If, however, terrestrial fire touches the dragon flames, the latter will immediately be extinguished.

As long as the dragon has moisture in the form of water or clouds surrounding its body, it retains its marvelous powers of motion and of mutability, but when this moisture dries up, the dragon becomes powerless and dies.

It is said that the blood of some dragons is red; of others, black. Rubies are often supposed to be petrified drops of the red variety.

We are informed of the remarkable fact that dragons change their bones periodically and as regularly as snakes shed their skins and deer their horns. Dragon bones are supposed to be buried in many high mountains, and their presence has much to do with the determination of fêng-shui. Lofty peaks that are frequently tipped with clouds or enveloped in mist are believed to contain the bones of some great dragon which attract to themselves the moisture of the passing clouds.

The saliva of the dragon, we are told, is purple in color, and is considered the most fragrant of all perfumes. It is said to be employed in the manufacture of a very valuable incense. "Dragon's saliva incense" was formerly sent as a tribute to the emperor by one of the western provinces.

One writer expresses a remarkable theory of the dragon's posthumous state. He says that when they die dragons turn into crabs. Dragons are punished for minor offenses, according to the will of heaven, by having their ears cut off; for greater offenses, by being sent to the earth, where they are exposed to the view of men in a state as if dead.

Three things of which dragons are exceedingly fond are bamboo trees, arsenic, and the flesh of swallows. The graceful branches of the bamboo are very pleasing to the eye of the dragon who, when there is no human being in sight, delights to lie under their shade and hear the wind rustling the leaves above. Arsenic, which is to mortal man a deadly poison, is food to the dragon. In fact, it is a favorite article of diet, and dragons grow fat upon it. The delicacy, however, for which the dragon has the greatest fondness, is swallows' flesh. Woe to the man who ever tries to cross a body of water in a boat after having eaten a dish of roasted swallows, for a peculiar fragrance, which dragons are always able to detect, will cling to his person. The man in the boat will be pursued by one of these animals, who will cause a storm to rise, the boat will be upset, and the unfortunate person precipitated into the water, where he will fall easy prey to the ruler of the sea. Under ordinary conditions the dragon shows no fondness for human flesh, but with such provocation we are told that he should be considered entirely excusable.

At the autumnal equinox, according to one source, the majority of dragons descend into the sea where they hibernate for six months. In fact, the home of dragons is on the floor of the ocean where they dwell in beautiful palaces. At the vernal equinox dragons leave the sea and ascend again into the clouds. Destructive typhoons and equinoctial hurricanes along the coast, in the spring and autumn, are caused by the disturbance of the waters when the great animals thus enter or leave their maritime home.

THE "DRAGON SQUARE"

This insignia of rank was worn on a gown by the great statesman Li Hung Chung. All Manchu officials carried, upon the front and the back of their robes of state, richly embroidered squares like this. The gowns of civil officers bore pictures of birds, while those of military officials had animals. Each of the nine ranks in both series employed its own distinguishing emblem. The dragon was worn by the prime minister, by princes, and the emperor. Li Hung Chang was prime minister of China for twenty years. The threads are of gold and silver and the background is black satin.

THE "DRAGON DISK"

This exquisite design was the insignia worn by a prince of the imperial house of the Ching dynasty. The insignia of the prime minister was square like those of lower officials. Princes were distinguished by circular emblems. This dragon disk is eleven inches in diameter and is embroidered with gold and black.

CHAPTER EIGHT
HOW DRAGONS CONTROL THE FORTUNES OF MEN

The surface of the earth is believed to be covered with a network of invisible paths of the dragon known as Lung Mei. People who build their houses or find graves for their dead upon one of these courses are extremely fortunate. The ruling emperors, however, made efforts to prevent their subjects from occupying the positions upon such auspicious sites. When Chao Ming, the founder of the Sung dynasty, while still an unknown young man in reduced financial straits, was forced to move his father's bones, he carried them in a reed bag and buried them by accident upon one of these dragon paths. As a result of this fact, we are told, heaven smiled upon him and he himself not long afterward became an emperor.

Within the past few years, a young Chinese, who had been studying in Japan, committed suicide for political reasons while on his way across the ocean. Because he was so well beloved he was buried by his friends in a beautiful mountain valley on a dragon path. The Board of Rites in Peking, on hearing of this, ordered the grave removed, sending telegram after telegram to the local magistrates to have the coffin disinterred at once and taken to another spot. Since the Revolution, it is said that the student's body has been taken back to its first resting place.

When Chinese observe the natural phenomenon which in the West is commonly described as "the sun drawing up water," they say that what is seen is the dragon sucking up water to form the clouds.

When rain falls upon one man's field and not upon his neighbor's, or upon one half of a man's farm and not upon the other, one explanation which is advanced for this fact is that the line which marks the division of dry and wet land is directly beneath the boundary line of the territory governed by two different dragons. One sees fit to order rain when the other does not. The territories controlled by the different dragons are redistributed once each year, on the seventeenth of the third month, which is known as "Li Hsia," "The Festival of the Beginning of Summer."

A few amusing illustrations of the way in which dragon superstitions have been allowed to play a leading part in Chinese life have come to the writer's attention. A Tientsin district magistrate, about forty years ago, tried to make an outlet from the Pei River in order to turn off the water at the time of a flood. After spending too much money in what proved to be an unsuccessful effort, he jumped into the river and was drowned. The story goes that the flood immediately subsided and the official turned into a dragon. Shortly afterwards he was changed into a snake and was captured. This creature was carried in state into Tientsin City where it was placed in the dragon temple and was worshiped by the viceroy of Chihli province, who was none other than Li Hung Chang. This official later became prime minister and held that position for twenty years.

In the heart of Wuchang there is a steep hill which cuts the business part of the city into two sections. This hill is so steep that it is practically impossible to carry the traffic over it. Some Chinese claim the hill to be the dwelling place of a tortoise, others of a serpent, and still others of a dragon. Some years ago, when Chang Chih Tung was living in that city as viceroy of Hunan and Hupeh, he caused a tunnel to be cut through the hill so that communication from one business center to the other would be facilitated. Not long after this was completed, the viceroy began to suffer from a carbuncle on his neck. Chinese and foreign physicians alike failed in their attempts to cure him. At last a geomancer was consulted. "I know the reason for your Excellency's illness," he said without hesitation. "You have caused the dragon's haunt to be penetrated. Block up the tunnel in the hill and you will get well." The thing was done, the viceroy soon recovered, and faith in the dragon on the part of the people of Wuchang was more firmly established than ever. It might be added that since the Revolution the tunnel through the hill has again been opened.

Many years ago large numbers of the students of Hangchow City failed to pass the Chu Jen, or Master of Arts, Examination. The fact sorely puzzled the city magistrates, who lost much "face." No explanation could be found for this fact until a geomancer explained that a dragon living in the mountain range northwest of the city had no room to wag his head, and that a large section of one end of the range must be dug away before Hangchow students would be able to succeed. The geomancer's suggestion was carried out, the dragon was given the chance he desired, and it is needless to say that since that time all has been well.

EMPEROR KANG HSI ON THE DRAGON THRONE

Kang Hsi was the second emperor of the Manchu dynasty. He ascended the throne at the age of eight and ruled China for over sixty years. This portrait was once preserved in the imperial galleries of the Manchu rulers.

A Dragon Lantern

The fifteenth day of the first month of the Chinese year is known as the "Feast of Lanterns." For centuries Chinese in many parts of the country have observed the evening of the fifteenth with lantern parades. One of the most spectacular of the lanterns usually exhibited is made in the form of a huge dragon. Before the Republic was established dragon lanterns were not infrequently seventy-five to one hundred feet in length. These were supported by from twenty-five to thirty men. Occasionally those lanterns were used at other times of the year, more particularly on the fifth of the fifth month of the lunar calendar, a holiday known as the "Dragon Boat Festival."

CHAPTER NINE
THE HOLD OF THE DRAGON ON CHINA

The word "dragon" occupies a prominent place in the common phraseology of the country. Some illustrations of this fact are as follows:

Deaf people are called "*lung*," a character formed by the combination of the dragon and ear characters signifying a person with ears like a dragon (which we are informed is deaf).

The asparagus plant is known as "dragon's beard grass."

The gentian flower is called the "dragon's gall."

A common variety of pine is known as "dragon's tail pine," from the supposed similarity of its branches to the tail of the dragon.

Amaryllis lilies and also the blossoms of a certain locust tree are called "dragon's claw flowers." This is no doubt on account of the shape of the flower clusters.

Fire engines are called "water dragons."

Locomotives and water faucets are commonly designated as "dragon heads."

The keel of a ship goes by the name of the "dragon bone."

Water spouts are known as "dangling dragons." The name was probably given them by junkmen and fishermen who considered these to be the tails of dragons suspended from the clouds.

Spirited horses are said to have "dragon dispositions."

Betrothal certificates are known as "dragon-phœnix papers."

Wedding cakes are called "dragon-phœnix cakes."

The published list of Master of Arts graduates was known as the "Dragon-Tiger Register."

A large number of cities, prefectures, rivers, and mountains have the character "dragon" incorporated into their names. One of the largest rivers of Manchuria and one of its three provinces are named Hei Lung Kiang (Black Dragon River), because it is related that a large black dragon once made its appearance in its waters.

One of the most famous mountains of the province of Kiangsi is known as the "Dragon-Tiger Mountain."

A Dragon Column

This remarkable monolith stands near the entrance to the famous Ming Tombs, thirty miles north of Peking. A huge dragon, surrounded by clouds, wraps itself closely about the tall shaft. There are two of these columns at the Ming Tombs, one on either side of the Spirit Road. The five-clawed dragons symbolize the imperial nature of the extensive cemetery, where are buried thirteen emperors, each in his massive mausoleum.

THE GATEWAY TO THE DRAGON WELL

Situated four or five miles west of the city of Hangchow is the center of the district that gives its name to what is perhaps the most famous tea in China. This is known as the "Lung Ching." The tea takes its name from a pool of water called "The Dragon Well." The walls of a monastery now surround the pool. This photograph shows the entrance to the temple grounds. The two characters over the arch form one of the best-known names in all China.

Perhaps the most popular kind of tea in China is the "Dragon's Well Tea." This received its designation from the fact that its original home was in a valley of that name. Among the hills on the farther shores of Hangchow's beautiful West Lake is nestled a monastery, on the estate of which is a pool of crystal-clear water. From the depths of this "well" a dragon was once seen to rise. The "Dragon's Well" is now the name of the monastery and also of the surrounding hills. Tea of this name, though it may never have grown near Hangchow, is as highly prized in distant Szechwan and in other distant parts of China as it is in the capital of Chekiang province.

In the excellent new encyclopedia recently issued by the Commercial Press, there are no less than 257 references to the dragon. Fifty-one of these are the names of cities or villages, twenty-four of mountains and rivers, and fifteen the names of flora of various genera.

The emperor's most reverential title was "The True Dragon," and in harmony with that idea the word "dragon" in the adjectival sense was used in names of all that had to do with his life and position. As an example of this his throne was the "dragon's seat," his hands the "dragon's claws," the pen he used was the "dragon's brush," the imperial robes were called "dragon's garments," and the imperial glance was known as "dragon's eyes."

The "Dragon Tablet" was the name given to the imperial tablet, which was worshiped during the Ching dynasty in every large temple and monastery in the land, and even in Mohammedan mosques. The inscription on the tablet read as follows: "To the reigning Emperor. May he live ten thousand years, ten thousand years, ten thousand times ten thousand years." The tablet received its name from the fact that it represented the Emperor, "The True Dragon," and because it bore at its top a dragon's head.

One insignia of official rank, until the recent Revolution, was the picture-square embroidered in gold and silver thread and worn on the front and back of official robes. The squares worn by civil officers bore the pictures of birds, while those of military officials were decorated with the pictures of animals; each rank and grade having its corresponding variety of bird or beast. The emperor, the princes, and the prime minister were allowed the special privilege of wearing the dragon on one of these embroidered squares.

THE DRAGON TABLET

During the Manchu dynasty, practically every Buddhist and Taoist temple of any size had an imperial dragon tablet in a prominent place upon the altar. Usually this stood before the image. The words it bore were these: "To the reigning emperor. May he live ten thousand years, ten thousand years, ten thousand times ten thousand years." In the gilded decoration about the characters three dragons twine themselves. Many such tablets may still be seen, although China has now been a Republic for ten years. This photograph was taken in Hangchow in March, 1922. The tablet stands on the altar in the Temple of the Great Buddha, which is situated upon the north edge of the West Lake.

A Dragon Boat Race in Foochow

This copy of an old engraving depicts a huge "dragon boat" passing gracefully up the Min River at Foochow. Twoscore rowers paddle the long craft, which glides swiftly up the river to the weird music of drums and gongs.

The round disk on the Chinese Dragon Flag, which is often pictured before the mouth of the dragon, is explained by some as a pearl, by others as a huge spider metamorphosed into a ball. We are repeatedly told in fables that dragons have a peculiar fondness for teasing spiders. A more satisfactory theory, however, is that the disk represents the sun. According to this explanation, the dragon is not trying to devour that heavenly body, as some would lead us to suppose, but is gazing with a great longing, for it desires to become like the sun in brilliance.

In referring to the Dragon Flag, the fact is worthy of notice that although this design appeared upon Chinese military banners through many centuries, the selection of the dragon emblem as a national insignia was of comparatively recent date. It is probable that the custom of foreign nations of using national emblems had a large part to play with the adoption of a national flag.

There is a feeling among many friends of China, and even among a few Chinese as well, that the effect of the Revolution and the passing of the Dragon Flag will very shortly kill out the dragon idea. This the writer believes is impossible. A belief that has gripped the nation for over forty centuries is not to be shaken even by a great revolution, which, though cataclysmic in itself, yet in relation to the ages which have passed, is little more than a ripple upon the surface of the sea of time. The dragon is neither a symbol of the

Manchu dynasty nor a type of absolute monarchy, and has nothing in common with either. The idea is distinctly a heritage of the Chinese race itself, and as such it will probably live as long as this people. It will survive at least until a generation after Western science has permeated and dominated every seaside village, every mountain hamlet, and every inland city, to the remotest bounds and limits of this vast Republic.

www.ingramcontent.com/pod-product-compliance
Ingram Content Group UK Ltd.
Pitfield, Milton Keynes, MK11 3LW, UK
UKHW040821280325
456847UK00003B/600